MONTEZUMA'S MISSING TREASURE

by

Anita Larsen

Illustrated by
Pamela Johnson

CRESTWOOD HOUSE
NEW YORK

Maxwell Macmillan Canada
Toronto

Maxwell Macmillan International
New York   Oxford   Singapore   Sydney

Library of Congress Cataloging-in-Publication Data
Larsen, Anita.

    Montezuma's missing treasure / by Anita Larsen. — 1st ed.
      p.   cm. — (History's mysteries)
    Includes bibliographical references and index.
    Summary: Discusses the mystery surrounding the lost treasure of the Aztec king Montezuma and presents three possible solutions.
    ISBN 0-89686-615-7
    1. Aztecs—History—Juvenile literature. 2. Mexico—History—Conquest, 1519-1540—Juvenile literature. 3. Montezuma II, Emperor of Mexico, ca. 1480-1520—Juvenile literature. 4. Cortés, Hernan, 1485-1547—Juvenile literature. 5. Treasure-trove—Juvenile literature. [1. Aztecs—History. 2. Indians of Mexico—History. 3. Mexico-History—Conquest, 1519-1540. 4. Cortés, Hernan, 1485-1547.]
I. Title. II. Series.
    F219.73.L37 1992
    972'.018—dc20
    [B]   91-19259
                                                                       CIP
                                                                            AC

Crestwood House
Macmillan Publishing Company
866 Third Avenue
New York, NY 10022

Maxwell Macmillan Canada, Inc.
1200 Eglinton Avenue East
Suite 200
Don Mills, Ontario M3C 3N1

Macmillan Publishing Company is part of the Maxwell Communication Group of Companies.

First edition

Printed in the United States of America

10 9 8 7 6 5 4 3 2 1

CONTENTS

▲▲▲▲▲▲▲▲▲▲▲▲▲▲▲▲▲▲▲▲▲▲▲▲▲▲▲▲▲▲▲▲▲▲

THE CASE OPENS

▲▲▲▲▲▲▲▲▲▲▲▲▲▲▲▲▲▲▲▲▲▲▲▲▲▲▲▲▲▲

It is early August 1521.

Hernan Cortes's Spanish conquistadores and their Indian allies are waging an all-out siege on the Aztec capital city, Tenochtitlan (tay-nohch-TEE-tlahn).

The Spanish are in the Valley of Mexico fighting "for God, glory and gold." They know gold is there. They've seen it before. In fact, they left a great deal of it behind when they were driven from Tenochtitlan the year before.

Cortes was often called "the greatest of the conquistadores." He said of Tenochtitlan that it was "the loveliest city in the world." The city itself was on an island in a large lake. It was connected to the mainland by hand-built roads called causeways. Cortes wanted to make it the capital of New Spain. But he knew from bitter experience that the Aztecs would not stop fighting until they had either won or had been destroyed.

The Spanish siege was slowly defeating the Aztecs. Indian bodies littered the streets that once were washed daily by a thousand-man crew. Some of the Aztecs had died fighting. Some had starved. Others ate rats, lizards, insects, grass, tanned hides, tree bark and lumps of clay, only to die of thirst. To quicken the Aztec defeat, the Spanish destroyed the four-mile-long aqueduct that brought water to the island city from the mainland.

Small Spanish ships called brigantines patrolled the lake surrounding the city. Brigantines were swift gunships powered by oars and sails. The guns easily destroyed the Aztecs' canoes.

By August 12, 1521, Tenochtitlan was almost entirely flattened. Cortes's army forced Aztec survivors into the last buildings still standing around the city's large marketplace.

The odds were hopeless, but the Aztecs fought on bravely. Cortes ordered a massive assault in order to force a surrender and, more important, to save lives. Cortes would need workers to build the capital of New Spain. He would need many Indian laborers.

But Cortes's Indian allies did not care about

saving Aztec lives. Centuries of Aztec domination made them bloodthirsty. On August 12 alone, 40,000 Aztecs were killed.

That day, Cortes called on Aztec leaders to discuss the possibility for peace. Some, including Chief Speaker Falling Eagle, tried to escape by canoe. Falling Eagle had become leader of the Aztecs after the death of the former Chief Speaker, Montezuma II. But Falling Eagle was captured and the fighting abruptly ended. An eerie silence replaced the sounds of battle.

That night a storm shattered the quiet of the battleground. Some thought the storm was the sound of Aztec gods shrieking as they disappeared forever into the surrounding mountains.

On August 14, Cortes gave his officers a victory banquet. Conquistadores dreamed that night of the gold they would reap the next day.

But they did not find gold. The greatest part of Montezuma's treasure should have been there—but it wasn't.

Cortes questioned Falling Eagle and other Aztec chiefs. They said they did not know where the gold was. The pile of booty was not big enough for the demanding soldiers.

Cortes feared mutiny. He ordered Falling Eagle

and another chief to be put in chains. Oil was smeared on the soles of their feet and set on fire. The other chief groaned in agony. But Falling Eagle clenched his teeth and bore the pain silently. Finally, Cortes stopped the torture and divided the loot.

The conquistadores were bitter. Where had Montezuma's treasure gone? No one knew then, and no one knows now.

THE CASE FILE

▲▲▲▲▲▲▲▲▲▲▲▲▲▲▲▲▲▲▲▲▲▲▲▲▲▲▲▲▲▲

AZTEC GLORY

The earliest Aztecs were poor wanderers. They often ran from their enemies. The Aztecs' only strength was their faith in their god Huitzilopochtli (weet-zeel-o-PO-tch-tly), or Hummingbird Wizard.

Hummingbird Wizard was not the tiny bird we know. This hummingbird was a fierce, blood-thirsty god. He was the lord of the sun, war and hunting. The priests said he would give the wandering Aztecs a sign when they reached their true home.

One day in the year that corresponded to the European year 1325, the Aztecs came to a shallow lake. The Aztecs kept such good calendars that the year can be pinpointed.

In the shallow lake were two islands. They were

little more than rock outcroppings ringed by mud flats. But the people could camp there and be safe from their enemies. The Aztecs built rafts and poled out to the islands.

On the shore they saw a prickly pear cactus growing in a cracked rock. A golden eagle gripped the plant with its talons, beating its wings for balance. From the bird's beak dangled a dead rattlesnake. This was the long-awaited sign!

The Aztecs stayed. They built the mud flats into gardens and fields. The islands were tied together by these gardens and fields and became Tenochtitlan, their capital city. Gradually, the Aztecs conquered the surrounding tribes and demanded large tributes, or taxes, from them. Aztec merchants traded far and wide, using people as pack animals. By the time the Spanish came in 1519, the Aztecs ruled the Valley of Mexico and beyond. The Valley of Mexico is the area around today's Mexico City.

The Aztecs were primitive in many ways, but they developed laws. Aztec justice was harsh but fair. People who lied had their lips cut off. Commoners seen drunk in public were beaten to death or strangled in front of the young men as a lesson. Drunken noblemen were drowned in private. A corrupt judge or official was punished more severely than an ordinary person for the same offense. The Aztecs thought those who had great authority should have an exemplary respect for law. Their code did not include European-style torture. No Aztec could mistreat another person to gain information or money.

"DIVINE WATER"

War was the way of the Aztecs' gods. Each night, Hummingbird Wizard, god of the sun, battled Smoking Mirror, god of night. When dawn came, the Aztecs knew that Hummingbird Wizard had defeated the dark. The Aztecs depended on Hummingbird Wizard to bring the sun their crops needed to grow.

The priests had seen that the heart of a living person pumped blood. The heart of a dead person did not. To them, blood became the key to life. Like people, the gods needed blood—"divine water"—to live.

The gods were offered human blood. Sacrifices were made on top of the great pyramid of Hummingbird Wizard. A war prisoner was held down on a stone platform while the high priest cut out his heart and held it up to the sun. The beating heart sprayed out blood that fed the sun.

Some Aztecs even offered themselves for sacrifice. Dying for their god was seen as an honor. Aztecs thought they would become gods if they died in sacrifice. War and blood rituals were necessities to the Aztecs.

THE ANGRY YOUNG LORD

Montezuma II became Chief Speaker of the Aztec empire in 1502. The Chief Speaker was the leader of the Aztecs in every way—religious, civil and military. Under Montezuma, the empire grew. His name means Angry Young Lord, and he had earned his name. A courageous general, he led his armies in person. He was also the empire's chief priest.

As the Aztecs' leader, Montezuma had complete power. He also had great responsibility to his people. Everything that happened in Aztec life was determined by a god, so Montezuma spent hours studying sacred scrolls.

In 1519, runners brought alarming news to Montezuma. Strange-looking people had come to their land. They had white skins and black beards. There was only one explanation, Montezuma thought. The strangers were gods.

Montezuma based his explanation on a legend about the god Quetzalcoatl (KA-yt-zal-co-atl), or

Feathered Serpent. This was one of the creators of the Aztec people. He was mightier even than Hummingbird Wizard. Feathered Serpent was the god of wisdom, the creator of the calendar and the inventor of farming. This god did not approve of human sacrifice.

Demons had driven Feathered Serpent from the Valley of Mexico. According to legend, Feathered Serpent had promised to return in the year One Reed, which was 1519 according to the European calendar. When he came back, he would overthrow those who sacrificed humans and rule Mexico till the end of time. It was said that sometimes Feathered Serpent appeared in the form of a white-skinned man with a bluish black beard.

THE "HOLY BANDITS"

The strangers were Hernan Cortes and his Spanish conquistadores. They weren't gods. But they believed they were soldiers of God—religious crusaders in the New World.

Cortes was an inspired and determined leader. He let no one stop him. He came from the Spanish province of Extremadura, a region of small farms and great poverty. He left school early and, by the time he was 19, had landed on the New World island of Hispaniola. Hispaniola today is divided between Haiti and the Dominican Republic. As a settler there, he was offered land and enough Indian slaves to farm it. According to Spanish records, he said, "Land? I don't want land. I didn't come here to till the soil like a peasant. *I came for gold!*"

When he got hungry, he took the land. He did well in the years that followed. Then he had a dream in which brown-skinned people bowed before him and called him prince. The dream told Cortes that God intended greater things for him.

In 1519, when he was 34, Cortes joined a small slave-hunting expedition. It left from Havana, Cuba, and sailed the uncharted waters to the Yucatan Peninsula. The only friendly natives they met there wore gold jewelry. The natives said the gold was from farther west, a place called Mexico. The word "Mexico" soon became to the Spanish another name for "gold."

Cortes immediately gathered men to go to Mexico. He sought battle-hardened men in their twenties and thirties. He wanted conquistadores, men who would fight as if God was on their side.

On February 10, 1519, Cortes and his conquistadores set sail for Mexico. Along the way, Cortes used interpreters to help him communicate with

the Indians. In the process, he discovered how to fight them.

The conquistadores' first battle was on March 13. They fought the Tabascan Indians. Although vastly outnumbered, Cortes did not retreat. Instead, he attacked. Indian warriors were brave, but their weapons were primitive and they were not organized to fight as a unit. Cortes's men were disciplined and followed a battle plan. This first fight became a model for Cortes's later battles.

The conquistadores' horses sealed the victory. The Tabascans had never seen a horse. They thought the horses were supernatural beings. They thought that animal and rider were a single warrior with the might of a god.

The Tabascan chiefs asked for peace. They offered Cortes gifts, including a woman named Malinali. She knew many Indian languages. She became Cortes's chief interpreter and his companion.

When Malinali became a Christian, she took the name Marina. The conquistadores called her Doña Marina, which meant honorable lady Marina. Without Doña Marina's help, Cortes would probably not have conquered Mexico.

"HEART MEDICINE"

Once Montezuma had heard the news about the strangers, he sent his Jaguar Knights to find the "water houses," as they called Cortes's ships. They brought gifts for Cortes, and Doña Marina welcomed them aboard. But Cortes ordered a cannon fired to show his disapproval of the gifts. He was not really angry. He wanted more from Montezuma.

When Montezuma heard the report from this meeting, he was sure that Feathered Serpent had returned. Montezuma hoped bribery or magic would send the god back home.

Montezuma sent another delegation to Cortes. This one was led by Tendile, his most trusted officer. It included 4,000 unarmed men. Priests went with burning incense. Servants carried a huge feast.

The Spanish were happy to see the fresh food. But when the priests threw a slave on his back, cut out his heart and sprinkled his blood over the meal, they were sickened. The priests were honoring the godlike Spanish with "divine water." They were also testing them to see if these men were really sent by Feathered Serpent.

The conquistadores' horrified reaction told the

Aztecs that Feathered Serpent had indeed returned. Aztec magic was nothing against this god's power.

A fresh meal was brought, along with more gifts. Now the Spanish were elated. The gifts were beyond their wildest dreams. Cortes gave Tendile a few worthless gifts in return. He said he would visit Montezuma in his capital and thank him in person for his generosity. He added that the Spanish suffered from a disease of the heart that could only be cured by gold. He said gold was "heart medicine."

But Tendile did not want Cortes to visit Montezuma. Tendile left and returned a week later with more gifts. He told Cortes that the road to Tenochtitlan was long and dangerous. He said there was not enough food in the city to feed such honored guests. He suggested that Cortes and his men take the gifts, get in their water houses and sail home. Sailing home was not what Cortes had in mind.

CRUSADING TO TENOCHTITLAN

Cortes's plan was to find Tenochtitlan and take the Aztecs' gold. He didn't know where the city was, but he set out anyway. He fought many battles along the way. Victory brought him the information he needed. Victory also brought him Indian allies. For years tribes had been forced to pay tribute to the Aztecs. They were eager to help the Spanish overthrow them.

Cortes's army didn't have an easy journey. But on the morning of November 5, 1519, they arrived at Tenochtitlan.

Hearing about Cortes's conquests, most Aztecs now believed the Spaniard was truly Feathered Serpent. The only one who didn't think so was Montezuma's younger brother. He wanted to fight the Spanish.

Montezuma ignored his brother's advice and prepared to greet the bearded god. Tens of thousands of Aztecs turned out to see him. As the Spaniards marched across the causeway into Tenochtitlan, awed Aztecs happily greeted them.

Montezuma appeared and bowed to Cortes. He called him lord and invited him to take possession of his throne in Mexico.

Montezuma took Cortes and his soldiers to a palace that had belonged to his late father, Lord Water Monster. It was more luxurious than any palace the Spanish had ever seen. Montezuma offered to let the Spaniards stay there.

The next day, the Spanish saw an even richer

palace. This was the palace of Montezuma. It was actually a small, self-contained city. Over 3,000 guards and servants worked in hundreds of rooms grouped around three courtyards. The first floor held the fabled "halls of Montezuma." These were huge rooms used for public ceremonies, law courts and the treasury. There was even a well-kept zoo, something still unheard of in Europe.

A week later Cortes asked Montezuma for a guided tour of the city. The market square was almost twice as large as any in Europe. From the roof of Hummingbird Wizard's temple, Cortes had a bird's-eye view of the city. His military mind calculated a possible escape route—if he needed it.

Inside the temple, Cortes saw the statue of fierce Hummingbird Wizard. The walls around it were smeared with crusted blood. Skulls of victims lined racks. The temple smelled like a slaughterhouse.

Cortes was angry. Outside, in the fresh air, he told Montezuma he wanted to set up a cross and a statue of the Virgin Mary in one of the temples.

Now it was Montezuma's turn to be angry. The Spaniard and the Aztec began to fear each other.

THE GOLD!

On November 14, 1519—nine days after they'd

entered the city—Cortes, Doña Marina and a small group of Spanish officers went to speak with Montezuma. They asked the Chief Speaker to come and live with them in Lord Water Monster's palace as a gesture of goodwill. But Cortes had something else in mind—securing the Aztec's gold. Montezuma refused. Hours of argument followed. At last, Doña Marina told Montezuma that he could come with them peacefully or be killed on the spot.

Montezuma went with them. He had been kidnapped, pure and simple. His entire court came with him.

In the next weeks, a strange friendship grew between Montezuma and his jailers. After all, Cortes promised his soldiers gold, but Montezuma simply gave it to them. The captive ruler himself showed the Spanish the public treasure house and his own personal treasure in the zoo. The Spanish seized the treasure and carried it back to Lord Water Monster's palace.

AZTEC REVOLT

In April 1520 the conflict between Montezuma and Cortes went a step further. Cortes and ten men stormed Hummingbird Wizard's temple and attacked the idol. Cortes demanded that all the idols

be taken down and that the temples be scoured clean of blood.

After the temples had been cleaned, Montezuma called Cortes to him. He told Cortes that Aztec priests had asked the gods to help them destroy the Spanish. Montezuma suggested that Cortes leave to avoid disaster.

Cortes said he could not leave because he had no ships. But Montezuma unrolled a scroll that showed that other Spanish forces had landed.

Cortes knew these were forces sent from one of his enemies in Cuba to capture him. Cortes decided to lead a surprise attack on this force. He left 150 soldiers under the command of Pedro de Alvarado to guard the capital and protect Montezuma. He ordered Alvarado not to provoke a fight.

Cortes's surprise attack was successful. He added 1,300 soldiers, 86 horses and over 30 cannons to his own forces.

When Cortes returned, he discovered he would need those reinforcements because Alvarado had not followed the order to avoid fighting. On May 16, 1520, a large number of Aztecs had gathered for a ceremonial dance. Alvarado and his small force got jittery when they saw the large crowd. They trapped and killed thousands of unarmed dancers.

This was called the Alvarado Massacre.

The Aztecs' grief at this outrage soon turned to fury. The enraged Aztecs swarmed around Lord Water Monster's palace and trapped Alvarado's forces inside.

Alvarado took Montezuma up to the roof. He put a dagger to the Chief Speaker's throat and ordered him to calm the crowds. But the people had turned against Montezuma. They thought he had sided with the Spanish.

A flurry of Aztec attacks on the palace went on for the next week. Then news of Cortes's victory came. The Aztec chiefs calmed the crowds. Their plan was to let Cortes come back to find a city in peace. Then they would kill *all* of their Spanish enemies at the same time.

Cortes returned to Tenochtitlan on June 24, 1520. He brought his new forces with him. He sensed a strange quiet in the city. He knew Spanish food supplies were running low.

The market had been closed since Alvarado's Massacre. Cortes ordered Montezuma to open it, but Montezuma said he was no longer the Aztecs' Chief Speaker. That office was usually passed on to the younger brother of the former speaker. Montezuma knew that his brother had long wanted

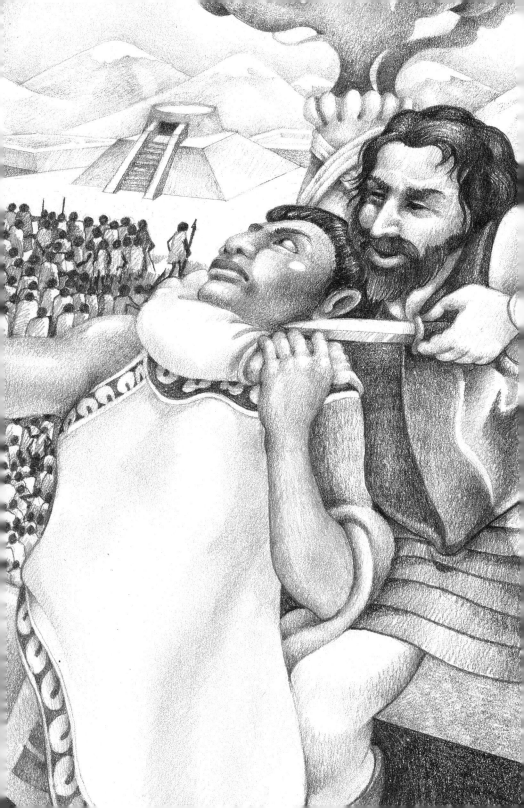

to fight the invaders. Now he tried to help his people in the only way left. He told Cortes to send for someone the rebels respected, like his younger brother.

Cortes did, not knowing the impact his action would have.

The next morning, the Aztecs mounted a huge attack. Their weapons were no match for the Spaniards' steel weapons and metal armor. Aztec armor was a shield of wood and animal hide, a wooden helmet and layers of cotton padding. But they could hurl rocks with lethal aim. One rock paralyzed two fingers of Cortes's left hand.

"LA NOCHE TRISTE"

The revolt continued. The Spanish lost 50 to 60 men a day to death or injury. Even with his reinforcements, Cortes knew that the Aztecs vastly outnumbered his dwindling forces. He told Montezuma that if he persuaded the Aztecs to stop fighting, the Spaniards would leave the city forever.

Montezuma dressed in his finest outfit, as if this was to be the last time his people would see him. He went to the roof. There was a silence as the former ruler looked at his people. He spoke, then listened to others speak from the crowd. Then the angry Aztecs threw stones. One struck Montezuma on the head, another on the arm, a third on the leg.

The Spanish carried him to his room. Surgeons revived the unconscious man and bandaged his wounds. Montezuma tore off the bandages. Three days later, on June 29, 1520, he died.

Now the Spanish had only two choices: Get out or die. Cortes planned an escape. The shortest causeway out of the city was two miles long. The Aztecs had removed the eight bridges spanning its defensive gaps. That was no problem for the cavalry. Men on horseback could jump the gaps or swim across the canal. The problem was getting out the infantry and their gear. Cortes asked his carpenters to build a portable bridge to span the widest gap. He planned to use a single portable bridge that could be moved from one gap to the next until the army got across.

At sunset on June 30, 1520, Cortes had Montezuma's treasure brought from storage and heaped in the main hall of Lord Water Monster's palace. He had the treasure melted and reshaped into gold bars and chains.

The Spanish king's share of the treasure was packed on eight lame horses. Cortes's servants would carry his share. Of the rest, each soldier could have what he could carry. Soldiers stuffed gold into their pockets and packs. Some fit three gold bars inside their helmets. But most of the gold was left behind.

Toward midnight, the Spanish slipped quietly into the empty streets. Patchy fog covered the ground near the lake, hiding them. The portable bridge worked perfectly. The army started across, elated at their luck. The first troops made it safely to the mainland.

Then their luck changed. A woman filling a water jug shouted an alarm. Instantly Aztec warriors attacked the Spanish from all sides. The portable bridge got stuck in the first gap. The Spanish army panicked. Soldiers in the rear pushed forward. Those in the front toppled over the edge of the next gap into the canal.

Nearly all those who fell into the water died. Some were dragged under by the weight of the gold they carried. Others were crushed by the soldiers and baggage that fell on them. Many others were dragged out by Aztec warriors to be sacrificed to Hummingbird Wizard. The rear guard was almost entirely wiped out.

Alvarado was one of the lucky few to survive. His horse was killed under him. He was thrown off, then ran toward the gap. He thrust his spear into

the water and pole-vaulted in full armor across the gap. That spot is now called "Alvarado's Leap." The pregnant Doña Marina also survived, tired but unharmed.

But 850 Spaniards and over 4,000 of their allies died. All but 24 of their 95 horses were killed. All the cannons were lost. Most of their weapons, ammunition and all their food was lost. Many millions of dollars worth of gold sank to the bottom of the lake.

For the Spanish, it was indeed *La Noche Triste,* the night of sadness. Cortes himself wept, standing by a cypress tree.

CORTES SPRINGS A TRAP

Cortes's conquistadores retreated. Six months later they again attacked the Aztecs.

This time thousands of Indian warriors from other tribes joined Cortes. He had also recruited 70,000 Indian laborers to carry supplies, build roads and do whatever the army needed. He had had 13 brigantines built in such a way that they could be dismantled, then reassembled at the Lake of the Moon. On December 26, 1520, Cortes's army began to march back to Tenochtitlan.

A lot had changed there since *La Noche Triste.*

The new Chief Speaker had died from the effects of smallpox, a European disease even Cortes had not realized he had left behind. The Indians had no resistance to the disease. It killed thousands.

A young and capable Chief Speaker had been elected. He was Cuauhtemoc (kwow-TA-y-moc), or Falling Eagle.

Falling Eagle ignored Cortes's offers of peace. He stockpiled food in public warehouses. He sent the heads of Spaniards and horses taken during *La Noche Triste* to the surrounding tribes to prove the Spanish weren't gods. He said that any tribes joining the Aztecs would not have to pay any more tribute.

By late April, Cortes's army had reassembled the brigantines and dug a canal. They began outfitting and arming the ships, then launched them. By the end of May, the Spanish had destroyed the aqueduct that brought water to Tenochtitlan.

On June 1, Cortes's fleet sailed. A thousand Aztec war canoes appeared. The Spanish ships cut through them. Spanish soldiers leaned over the ships' decks to stab the Aztec warriors who foundered in the water. Then Cortes deployed his troops for an attack on Tenochtitlan.

At dawn on June 30, 1521, the first wave of the

Spanish forces attacked. They were defeated. Afterward, the Aztecs left the battlefield to worship and make sacrifices of captured soldiers. When the Spanish saw their comrades being sacrificed, they wept.

At that point, Cortes decided to lay siege upon Tenochtitlan. At the end, the city was buried under 30 feet of rubble and human corpses.

As time went on, the Lake of the Moon was almost entirely filled in. Eventually, a new city would rise on the ruins—the Very Noble, Notable and Most Loyal City of Mexico, today's Mexico City. The entire Aztec civilization was destroyed. And the Aztec gold was lost forever. What happened to it?

You have just read the known facts about one of HISTORY'S MYSTERIES. To date, there have been no more answers to the mysteries posed in the story. There are possibilities, though. Read on and see which answer seems the most believable to you. How would you solve the case?

SOLUTIONS

▲▲▲▲▲▲▲▲▲▲▲▲▲▲▲▲▲▲▲▲▲▲▲▲▲▲▲▲▲▲

THE TREASURE WAS BURIED

Before Montezuma died, he recognized the deceitfulness of the Spanish. He turned the control of his empire over to those who opposed the Spanish. Between *La Noche Triste* and the return of Cortes's forces, two Chief Speakers saw to it that the Aztec gold was taken north and hidden. In the same way that their vast trade network was run, Aztec porters carried away the treasure, bit by bit, on their backs.

Where did they hide the gold?

One account says the caravan went north 275 leagues, then turned west into high mountains. There, the gold was hidden in a cave. A league is about three miles, so this explanation would place the gold somewhere in the Sierra Madre range. No one has yet found it.

Another account says the caravan went much farther north, into what is today Arizona, New Mexico and Utah. There is some evidence that the Aztecs traded with the Pueblo Indians who lived there.

This explanation has influenced many treasure hunters. A report from 1876 says that a young Mexican came to Taos, New Mexico. He had information that led him to a cave on Taos Mountain. He emerged from the cave and ran to a cliff to shout to onlookers that he'd found the Aztec gold. Suddenly, a powerful wind blew him off the cliff, dashing him onto the rocks below. No one else has ever found the cave. The land has now been returned to the control of the Taos Pueblo.

Another account centers on the town of Kanab, Utah. In 1914 a prospector named Freddie Crystal came to Kanab. He talked about looking for Aztec gold. He'd found a book in Mexico that showed a canyon marked by carved symbols. He'd come to Utah, where he thought he might find the canyon. He left Kanab, returning in 1922 to report that there was such a canyon on White Mountain. He said he had found a giant tunnel that had been carefully sealed a long time ago. The whole town went out to break into the tunnel. All they found was rock.

Just because these searches failed doesn't mean the Aztecs didn't bury their treasure far to the north of their capital. Perhaps people just haven't looked in the right place yet.

THE TREASURE WAS SUNK

The conquistadores tortured Falling Eagle to get information about the missing treasure. Falling Eagle said only that much gold had been thrown into the water.

The bottom of the Lake of the Moon was marshy. The best divers were put to the task of bringing up the gold. They could find only a few pieces of no great value. In the muddy bottom, divers could not even find the gold that was lost during *La Noche Triste!*

The only object of real worth was found in a pond in Falling Eagle's garden. It was a large calendar wheel of pure gold.

Tenochtitlan was eventually leveled. Over the years, the Lake of the Moon was filled in. What is now Mexico City was built on top of it. Perhaps Montezuma's treasure is now buried under the streets of Mexico City.

THE TREASURE WAS SPENT

After *La Noche Triste,* Cortes was determined to conquer the Aztecs. He gathered an army, paying for weapons and horses with the gifts Montezuma had given him before the two met. No price was too great for a cannon. Any Spanish soldier who came to Cortes with a horse was given a pocketful of gold.

Meanwhile, Falling Eagle was preparing for Cortes's return. He recruited support and supplies from surrounding villages. He displayed the heads of fallen Spanish soldiers and their horses to show that the invaders were not gods. Falling Eagle gave away the gold that the Spanish had left behind in order to enlist support. Bribery was not foreign to the Aztecs.

The gold that the Spanish left behind in Lord Water Monster's palace was used to pay for the defense of Tenochtitlan.

CLOSING THE CASE FILE
▲▲▲▲▲▲▲▲▲▲▲▲▲▲▲▲▲▲▲▲▲▲▲▲▲▲▲▲▲▲

As soon as Tenochtitlan fell, Cortes ordered the Aztec chiefs to build a Spanish-style city on the same site. He called the conquered territory New Spain. The Indians provided both labor and materials.

Today's Mexico City is built in the style of a Spanish city. Beneath it lie the ruins of Tenochtitlan.

Some bits of Tenochtitlan still remain, though. The cypress tree where Cortes wept after *La Noche Triste* is still alive. Not far from this tree is a square with a plaque set in the wall. The plaque begins with the words, "The Place Where the Slavery Began." It marks the site where Falling Eagle was made prisoner when the Spanish captured Tenochtitlan.

In fact, a European form of slavery did begin that

THE PLACE WHERE SLAVERY BEGINS

day for most Indians. But not all Indians were enslaved. As Montezuma lay on his deathbed, Cortes promised to care for the royal children. Montezuma's heirs received land and enough people to work it. Montezuma's two surviving daughters became Christians and married Spanish noblemen. Their descendants still trace their roots to the Aztecs' Angry Young Lord.

Cortes's soldiers were given land and workers in place of the gold they'd been promised. Land and workers were also given to later Spanish settlers. Some of the new landowners tortured and terrorized the Indians.

But the Indians' greatest loss was their traditional way of life. The world they knew ended when the Spanish came. Soon their traditional beliefs were replaced by Christianity. Tribute paid to the Aztecs was replaced by tribute paid to Cortes.

Cortes returned to Spain in 1540. He wanted two things: a higher title than the one he was offered, Marquis of the Valley of Oaxaca, and a new military assignment. He failed to secure either. He was now 63 and felt old. He wanted to go home to Mexico. While waiting for a ship to take him back, he became ill. He died in his bed in Spain on December 2, 1547.

Cortes's body was taken back to New Spain. He was buried in a church near the spot where he and Montezuma first met. Perhaps Montezuma's gold is buried beneath them both. When new buildings in Mexico City are begun, Aztec artifacts are often found in the excavations.

CHRONOLOGY

▲▲▲▲▲▲▲▲▲▲▲▲▲▲▲▲▲▲▲▲▲▲▲▲▲▲▲▲▲▲▲▲▲▲▲

1325   Aztecs settle in the Valley of Mexico.

1502   Montezuma II becomes Chief Speaker.

1519   February 10, Cortes begins his conquest.
        November 5, Cortes enters Tenochtitlan.
        November 14, Montezuma is kidnapped.

1520   May 16, Alvarado Massacre.
        June 25, Aztec revolt.
        June 29, Montezuma dies.
        June 30, *La Noche Triste.*
        December 26, Cortes's crusaders begin to
                    return to Tenochtitlan.

1521   April 28, Siege brigantines are launched.
        May 26, The Aztec aquaduct is
                destroyed.
        August 13, Tenochtitlan falls.

1547   December 2, Cortes dies.

RESOURCES

▲▲▲▲▲▲▲▲▲▲▲▲▲▲▲▲▲▲▲▲▲▲▲▲▲▲▲▲▲▲▲▲

SOURCES

Burland, C. A. *Montezuma: Lord of the Aztecs*. New York: G. P. Putnam & Sons, 1973.

Miller, Robert Ryal. *Mexico: A History*. Norman, Okla: Univ. of Oklahoma Press, 1985.

Natella, Arthur A. *The Spanish in America, 1513-1974*. Dobbs Ferry, N.Y.: Oceana, 1975.

FURTHER READING FOR YOUNG READERS

Beck, Barbara L. *The Aztecs*. 2nd ed; rev. New York: Franklin Watts, 1983.

Marrin, Albert. *Aztecs and Spaniards*. New York: Atheneum, 1986.

von Hagen, Victor W. *The Sun Kingdom of the Aztecs*. New York: World Publishing Co., 1958.

INDEX

▲▲▲▲▲▲▲▲▲▲▲▲▲▲▲▲▲▲▲▲▲▲▲▲▲▲▲▲▲▲▲▲▲▲▲▲